Bobbo Goes to School

For Clare Hall-Craggs and family

First U.S. edition 2013

Library of Congress Cataloging-in-Publication Data is available.

Library of Congress Catalog Card Number pending

ISBN 978-0-7636-6524-1

12 13 14 15 16 17 LEO 10 9 8 7 6 5 4 3 2 1

Printed in Heshan, Guangdong, China

This book was typeset in Century Old Style.
The illustrations were done in gouache.

Candlewick Press
99 Dover Street
Somerville, Massachusetts 02144

visit us at www.candlewick.com

Bobbo Goes to School

Shirley Hughes

CANDLEWICK PRESS

It was Monday morning, and Mom was loading the washing machine. Lily wasn't helping. She was hiding Bobbo among the towels and sheets.

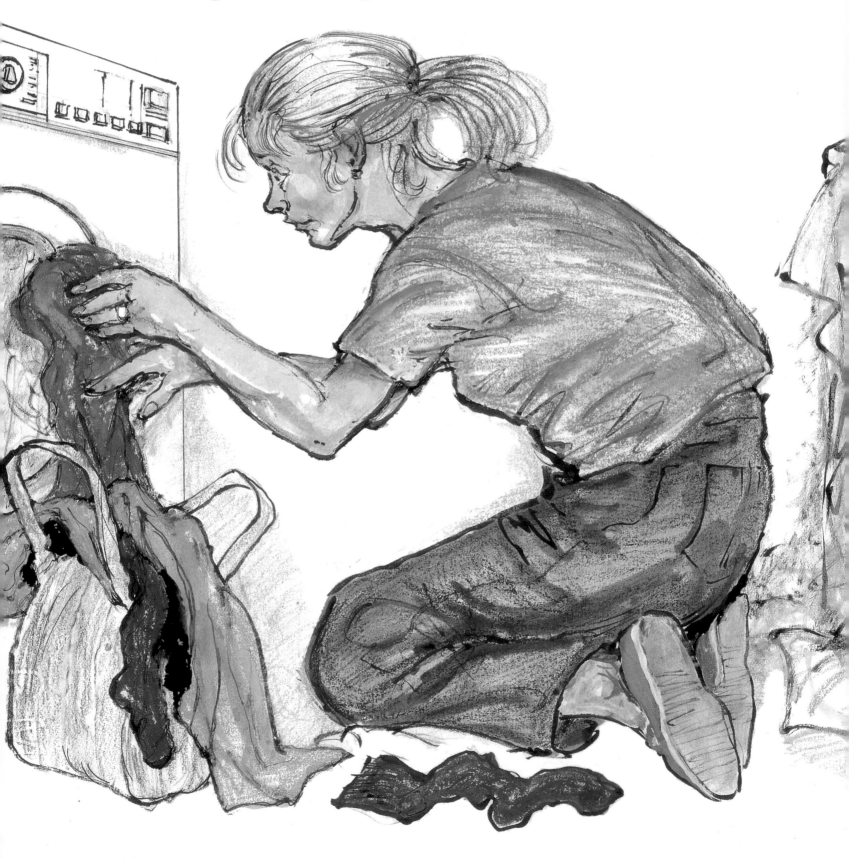

"Please stop that, Lily," said Mom,
"or I'll never get this done."

Lily stopped. But then she started to throw Bobbo into the air and catch him by the leg. Bobbo could tell it was going to be one of Lily's bad days.

After Mom had turned on the washing machine, it was time to go shopping. She pulled Lily's sweater over her head and pushed her arms into the sleeves. Lily did not help. She went all limp like a rag doll.

"Shall we take Bobbo?" said Mom. "I'm sure he'd like to come."

Lily stopped going limp, and together they looked for Bobbo. They found him hiding under a cushion. At last they were ready to set off.

While Lily and Bobbo were waiting on the sidewalk for Mom
to open up the stroller, they saw the school bus pull up.

The bus monitor helped the children jump aboard.
Then the driver closed the door.

Just as the bus was pulling away, Lily did
a dreadful thing. She swung Bobbo around
and around by his leg and threw him high
into the air — just like that! Bobbo flew up
headfirst and landed smack-dab on the roof
of the bus, just as it was pulling away.

Lily and Mom were too shocked to move. They both stood there and watched as the bus gained speed and disappeared.

"Bobbo! I want him back!" wailed Lily.

But it was too late. Bobbo was gone.

Lily and Mom rushed back indoors, and Mom got on the phone right away. She spoke to a lady at the school and told her that Bobbo would soon be arriving on top of the school bus and would they please rescue him.

Lily cried and cried. "He might fall off and get run over!" she howled. "And I won't see him ever again!"

In fact Bobbo had not fallen off. He was lying faceup, rushing along very fast and looking up at the sky. Sometimes he slipped a bit, but he stayed aboard. This was all rather exciting for Bobbo. He had never traveled on a bus without Lily before.

Down below, the children laughed and talked and looked out the bus windows. They had no idea that Bobbo was riding on the roof of their bus.

Soon the bus arrived at school.
When the driver stopped near
the entrance, Bobbo went
flying straight into a bush.

It felt like being a bird. For a moment, Bobbo thought he *was* a bird. He felt rather tired after all this excitement, so he just lay there, swaying gently and wondering what would happen next.

What an extraordinary day this was turning out to be for Bobbo!

Back at home, Lily's day was going from bad to worse. Mom telephoned the school again.

But the lady who answered said that the driver had looked on top of the bus and no soft toy had been found there.

Lily wept. It was terrible to think
that she had thrown away her
oldest, dearest friend.

"I want Bobbo back now!"
she sobbed.

Meanwhile, as Bobbo was resting among the leaves,
the schoolchildren came out for recess.

A little girl named Natasha, who was playing by the bush
with her friend, found Bobbo and handed him to the teacher.

All the children crowded around and made a great
fuss over him. No one knew where he had come from.

So they took him to their classroom and put him in a special place on the Interest Shelf where he could see everything.

He sat there for the rest of the morning while the children
did counting and drew pictures and listened to a story.

When the lady in the school office heard that Bobbo had been found, she telephoned Mom and Lily and they drove to the school right away. Lily was allowed to go into the classroom to collect him. When she saw him on the Interest Shelf, she ran straight over and hugged him tight.

Then the teacher and children showed Lily what they had been doing with Bobbo.

They told her that they had been playing a game: they were trying to guess what his name was. Each of them had written their guess down.

Lily told them that none of them had gotten it right because his name was Bobbo!

She was very happy, and she thanked them and said good-bye.

"Oh, what a relief that we've found him!" said Mom when at last they arrived back home. "I think he liked it at school, and you'll like it too, Lily, when you're old enough to go there."

Lily was hugging Bobbo very tight, pressing her face against his nose. "I'll never, never throw you away again!" she whispered.

Bobbo didn't say anything.
Lily's bad day had turned out
well after all.